REAL LIVES
BASEBALL GREATS

edited by
Miriam Rinn

Troll

Cover illustration by Robert Papp

Copyright © 1999 by Troll Communications L.L.C.

All rights reserved. No part of this book may be reproduced or utilized in any form or by any means, electronic or mechanical, including photocopying, recording, or by any information storage and retrieval system, without written permission from the publisher.

Printed in the United States of America.   ISBN 0-8167-4934-5

10 9 8 7 6 5 4 3 2 1

Other books in the REAL LIVES series

Great Adventurers
Heroes & Idealists
Leaders of the People
Seekers of Truth
Women of Valor

TABLE OF CONTENTS

Babe Ruth 7

Lou Gehrig 17

Jackie Robinson 27

Willie Mays 39

Roberto Clemente 51

Index 62

Babe Ruth

It was game number three of the 1932 baseball World Series. The date was October 1, and the New York Yankees were playing the Chicago Cubs. It was the fifth inning, and the score was tied, 4–4. One of baseball's most dramatic moments was about to take place.

The great Yankee player, Babe Ruth, was at bat, and the Chicago pitcher, Charlie Root, was being very careful with every pitch he threw. He didn't want the top home-run hitter in the major leagues to blast the ball out of the stadium.

Ruth was just as determined to get a hit. He always enjoyed hitting and playing baseball, but today was special. The Chicago fans were booing and throwing things at him from the stands. He was angry at the Chicago players, too, who had been yelling insults at him since the start of the World Series.

Now the crowd was roaring for Root to strike out the Yankee slugger. The count was two balls and two strikes. One more strike and Ruth would be out. The players were screaming at him from the Cubs' bench. He glared at them, then turned and faced the pitcher. Suddenly, Ruth smiled and pointed toward the distant center-field fence. He seemed to be saying, "Throw me your best pitch. I'm going to hit it over that fence!"

On the next pitch, the Yankee star swung, the bat connected, and the ball flew high over the center-field fence, right where he had pointed! Ruth couldn't have placed the ball better if he had carried it there in his hands. It was also the longest hit in the history of Chicago's Wrigley Field. With that dramatic home run to inspire them, the Yankees went on to win the game, and the 1932 World Series.

George Herman Ruth, one of the greatest baseball players of all time, was born on February 6, 1895, in Baltimore, Maryland. He didn't get the nickname "Babe" until he began his professional baseball career. Before then, he was called George, or Little George, because his father was also named George.

Mr. and Mrs. Ruth were poor, uneducated people who moved from one apartment to another in a run-down Baltimore neighborhood. Mr. Ruth worked as a lightning-rod salesman, a wagon driver (in the days before there were automobiles), a laborer, a saloonkeeper, and a harness salesman, but no job ever lasted very long.

Kate Schamberger Ruth, Little George's mother, was in poor health most of the time. Although she gave birth to eight children, only two lived past childhood—George and his younger sister, Mamie. Mrs. Ruth tried to give the family a decent home, but she was simply unable to take good care of Little George. As soon as the young boy could walk, he was out roaming the streets. Sometimes he put together his own dinner from what little food was in the apartment, but on many days, he went without a solid meal. Baths and clean clothes were as rare in George's life as a decent meal. He survived those early years almost like a stray animal, alone and unwanted.

George's only real love and attention came from his mother's parents. The Schambergers fed their grandson when he came to visit, and gave him the affection he didn't get at home. Mr. and

Mrs. Schamberger were German immigrants who spoke only German, and Little George picked up their language quickly. In fact, he spoke German before he spoke English. Most of the English that he learned before he was school age was what he heard in the streets.

Mr. and Mrs. Ruth were not good parents, and most of the time they paid no attention to George at all. Between them, the Ruths made their son feel worthless and unloved. It was a childhood that a writer would later describe as "no childhood at all." Ruth agreed, and acknowledged, "I had a rotten start, and it took me a long time to get my bearings."

When George reached school age, his life remained the same. His parents said nothing when he didn't bother to go to school, so day after day, he roamed the streets with other aimless boys. They taught him to swear, to chew tobacco, to steal apples from fruit stands, and to fight. "I was a bum when I was a kid," Ruth said sadly, recalling those early years. "Looking back on my boyhood, I honestly don't remember being aware of the difference between right and wrong."

When George was six years old, his parents bought a saloon. George spent a lot of time there, even though it was a terrible place for a young boy. Late in the spring of 1902, a big fight broke out in the saloon, shots were fired, and the police were called. One of the officers learned that a small child was there when the shooting took place. Not only that, a neighbor told the officer, the boy was there at all hours of the day, and never went to school. When the police reported this, the proper authorities took action.

On June 13, 1902, Mr. Ruth and George took a trolley-car ride across the city of Baltimore and got off at St. Mary's Industrial School for Boys. The court had ordered the Ruths to place their son in the school for his own well-being. George was only seven-and-a-half years old, and the order said that he would have to stay at the school until his 21st birthday.

St. Mary's Industrial School for Boys was made up of six large, gray buildings, each standing three stories high. There was a broad playing field on the grounds, but it was little more than a bare, dusty area. Eight hundred boys were housed and cared for at the school. Some, like George, were sent there because they had been neglected at home. Some were orphans in need of shelter. Still others were runaways or boys who had gotten into trouble with the law. There were no real criminals at St. Mary's, just youngsters who needed care and guidance.

At first, George was homesick and unhappy, and he cried all the time. He hated having to wear the denim overalls that were the school uniform. The dormitory where he slept had 200 beds, and George found it a scary place to be. He missed his little sister, his grandparents, and his friends.

St. Mary's was run by Catholic brothers, but the school took in boys of all faiths. The only requirement was that the child need their help. The brothers were teachers, coaches, cooks, carpenters, painters, and craftsmen, and they taught any boy who was willing to learn. The brothers were friends and advisors who believed their main job was to turn out honorable, decent young men.

It took George a while to get used to the routine at St. Mary's. The boys went to bed at eight o'clock every night and got up at six every morning. After washing and dressing, they went to chapel. Chapel was followed by a breakfast of oatmeal, bread and butter, and a glass of milk. Classes started at seven-thirty and continued until lunch hour. Lunch was the main meal of the day, and it was always hot, fresh, and filling.

The cooking wasn't fancy at the school but it was nutritious, and the boys always had enough to eat. This was a change for some of them, including George, who had never been sure of when or where he would eat his next meal.

St. Mary's had boys as young as five and as old as 21. Until they reached the age of 14, the youngsters attended morning and afternoon classes. The older boys spent only their mornings in class, devoting the afternoons to learning a trade in order to prepare themselves for life as adults.

For boys of all ages, the late afternoons and all day Sunday were set aside for sports. These included football, soccer, handball, basketball, volleyball, foot races, boxing, wrestling, and ice skating, but the most important sport at St. Mary's was baseball. There were 43 teams at the school, and each one had a name, uniforms, and a regular playing schedule.

The brothers were just as enthusiastic about baseball as the boys. They were fans themselves, who enjoyed coaching and watching a good game. Even so, baseball and the rest of the sports program had another, more important purpose than just fun and exercise. Most of the boys, like George, hadn't been part of a team before. They didn't know how to play together, to help others, or to settle arguments except by fighting. The brothers used sports to teach self-discipline, honesty, fairness, team play, and how to win and lose.

As Little George settled into the daily routine, he found that St. Mary's wasn't such a bad place at all. For the first time in his life, George Herman Ruth was clean, well fed, and warmly dressed.

George never liked schoolwork, but at St. Mary's he did learn to read and write. When he first arrived, he could not recognize a single number or letter and barely spoke a complete English sentence. The other boys laughed at him because he had to attend classes with younger children. Their scorn made him feel stupid and unable to learn, and this feeling stayed with him all his life.

Afternoon sports didn't end until the supper bell rang. Then, after eating, the boys had band or choir practice, and time to go to the canteen. The canteen was a small building on the school grounds that sold candy, cakes, peanuts, and other snacks. The boys did not have money to spend, but they paid for snacks with credits earned by work they did around the school.

George liked candy and cake, and any other kind of sweet. Before he came to St. Mary's, these were rare treats, and now it seemed he could never get enough. Still, he always shared his snacks with friends. This generosity stayed part of Babe Ruth's character even when he was an adult. As a baseball star he earned a great deal of money, and he spent it freely on his friends.

George's huge appetite for food also stayed with him. Part of the Babe Ruth legend is the number of hot dogs he ate before, during, and after ball games; the gallons of ice cream he enjoyed in one sitting; and his meals that could have filled the stomachs of three normal eaters.

As much as young George liked food, there was something he liked even more. He loved playing baseball. The baseball field was the only place where he was a success. George struggled with reading and arithmetic. He was so homely that the other boys made fun of his face, and they laughed at the way he walked with his toes pointing inward. He was clumsy and forgetful, and he still felt lonely and unloved. But at baseball he was a natural. He could hit better than any other boy his age. He could throw and run and catch as if he had done nothing else since the day he was born.

George played the game 12 months a year. When it wasn't baseball season, some boys still used the bat and ball. If there weren't enough players for a regular game, they had a two-player game called "pokenins." One player was the batter. He stood in front of a wall, facing the pitcher. The batter kept hitting until the pitcher got him out. Then the boys changed places. When George Ruth pitched, he put out the other boy fast. When George was batting, he hit one pitch after another.

George's baseball abilities caught the attention of Brother Matthias, who was in charge of sports at the school. Brother Matthias, who stood over six feet tall and was a powerful man, didn't have to yell or raise his voice to be obeyed. The boys respected him because he was as fair as he was tough.

For George, Brother Matthias was a combination of father, friend, coach, and advisor. He realized that George could be helped through baseball and that the sport could be used to teach the boy discipline and pride in himself, and to win the admiration of others. With all this in mind, Brother Matthias began to concentrate on getting George to make the most of his gifts.

They spent hours together on the ball field, practicing every part of the game. Many years later, Babe Ruth said, "I always felt I could hit the ball, even the first time I held a bat. But Brother Matthias taught me some other things. He made me a pitcher and showed me how to field. He really knew the game of baseball and he loved it." Ruth described Brother Matthias as the greatest man he had ever known.

As George entered his teen years, his outstanding play won many games for St. Mary's and brought him the respect of the other boys. He still might have classes with young children, but it was a different story on the baseball diamond. There, he was placed with the oldest players at the school—and he was better than any of them.

When George reached his 14th birthday, he began to learn the shirtmaking trade. His part of the job was putting collars on shirts, for which he earned a canteen credit of six cents for each shirt. George enjoyed the work and became quite good at it. Even when he was the highest paid baseball player in America, he took pleasure in removing a worn collar from one of his expensive silk shirts and replacing it with a new collar. He didn't do it to save the cost of a new shirt. The world's greatest baseball player simply was proud of the skill that had never left him.

By the age of 16, George was almost six feet tall. Pictures of him as an adult show him as a heavy man, but as a boy he was thin. It was only when he grew older that he gained weight, reaching 215 pounds during the peak years of his career. Yet Babe Ruth's arms and legs remained slim. He never looked too muscular, but even as a youngster he was exceptionally strong.

Sixteen-year-old George played for one of the best teams at St. Mary's, the Red Sox. The school's top teams were part of a league with other schools in the Baltimore area, in which each team was named after a major-league baseball club. In 1912, when the Red Sox won the school championship, George was the team's catcher. At this time, however, Brother Matthias began developing the left-handed youngster into a pitcher. It wasn't long before Ruth was the finest pitcher St. Mary's had ever seen.

George's hitting was also extraordinary. Time and again he drove the ball more than 400 feet from home plate, which is more than most professional ballplayers can do. The teenager also hit over 60 home runs in one of his seasons with the St. Mary's Red Sox. That number would become significant during Ruth's professional career. In the 1927 season, he hit 60 home runs. It was a record that stood until Roger Maris, of the New York Yankees, hit 61 home runs in 1961. (Roger Maris had an important advantage. The 1961 season had 162 games, while the 1927 season had only 154 games.)

George Ruth was soon recognized as the best pitcher and hitter in the Baltimore high-school league. By 1913, when he was 18, his brilliance as a baseball player came to the attention of Jack Dunn. Mr. Dunn was the owner of the Baltimore Orioles, then a professional minor-league baseball team. Mr. Dunn watched the tall, strong teenager pitch one game, and that was enough to convince the team owner that the young man had a promising baseball future.

Jack Dunn was ready to give George a contract to pitch for the Orioles, but one problem stood in their way—Ruth was too young to sign a legal contract. Then one of the St. Mary's brothers found a solution. Mr. Dunn could become George's legal guardian and sign the contract for him. Mr. Dunn promised to care for George as if he were a son, and the papers were signed. On

February 27, 1914, George Herman Ruth left St. Mary's to join the Orioles for spring training.

On the ball field, George was an immediate success, but off the field, he wasn't nearly as sure of himself. He was dazzled by a world that was so different from St. Mary's. George's first elevator ride lasted for hours. When he was given five dollars for expense money, he felt rich. But the biggest thrill of all was learning that he could eat as much as he wanted, at the team's expense.

George's innocent behavior was funny to the veteran players, who teased him constantly. Finally an Oriole coach warned them, "You be careful with the teasing. This boy is one of Mr. Dunn's babes." The teasing stopped, but the nickname "Babe" stuck. From then on, George Herman Ruth always called himself Babe.

That spring saw the birth of one of baseball's greatest careers. During the next 22 years, Babe Ruth starred for the Boston Red Sox, New York Yankees, and Boston Braves. In that time, he set pitching and hitting records that lasted for many years. Some still stand unbroken.

The Babe, or the Bambino, as he was affectionately known, was more than baseball's brightest star. He was the symbol of the sport to millions of Americans. Wherever the Babe played, fans packed the stadium.

Babe Ruth finished his long career in the same magical style that had made him an American hero. On May 25, 1935, Babe's team, the Boston Braves, were playing the Pittsburgh Pirates at home, in Forbes Field. The aging slugger was tired and feeling sick. Everyone was saying he was through, that he had lost his ability to play, even to hit. Babe's pride, however, wouldn't let him go out looking bad. In the first inning of that game, he hit a two-run homer off Pirate pitcher Red Lucas. Two innings later, Ruth hit another two-run homer. This time the pitcher was Guy Bush. In the fifth inning, against Bush, Ruth hit a single to drive in another run.

In the seventh inning, Babe came to bat again. Bush was still pitching and no runners were on base. He threw the 40-year-old slugger a blazing fastball, and Ruth's bat connected for another home run! It was his third homer of the day, and the 714th of his magnificent career. It was also the kind of home run that had made Ruth a living legend. The ball traveled more than 600 feet. It sailed over the stadium roof in the right field and completely out of the ball park.

As Guy Bush, the Pittsburgh pitcher, later said, "I never saw a ball hit so hard before or since. He was fat and old, but he still had that great swing. Even when he missed, you could hear the bat go swish. I can't remember anything about the first home run he hit off me that day. I guess it was just another homer. But I can't forget that last one. It's probably still going."

Babe Ruth died on August 16, 1948, at the age of 53. He was one of the first players elected to baseball's Hall of Fame. When he died, baseball fans everywhere mourned the passing of a true sports legend.

Lou Gehrig

The Philadelphia fans settled into their seats for the baseball game between their home team, the Athletics, and the New York Yankees. The sky was cloudless on that June 3, 1932, afternoon. It was a perfect day for baseball. It would turn out to be an unforgettable one, too.

The first Yankee batter of the game got on base. The next batter made an out, and the batter after that—the great Babe Ruth—struck out. This brought Lou Gehrig up to bat. The Philadelphia pitcher, George Earnshaw, wound up and threw the ball. Gehrig swung, there was a loud *smack*, and the baseball sailed far over the left-field fence. It was a home run. Now the Yankees led, 2–0.

The teams battled on, and every time Philadelphia tied the score or went ahead of the Yankees, Lou Gehrig came to bat. Each of those times, his hitting put the Yankees in front again. He hit his second home run of the game in the fourth inning, and his third home run in the fifth inning.

In the seventh inning, the first two Yankees to bat hit home runs. Philadelphia's manager, Connie Mack, decided to take Earnshaw out of the game and replace him with relief pitcher Roy

Mahaffey. As Earnshaw approached the Philadelphia dugout, Manager Mack said, "Watch closely. I want you to see how Mahaffey pitches to Gehrig." Earnshaw, Mack, both teams, and thousands of fans watched closely. Mahaffey reared back and threw his best pitch to Gehrig. Gehrig, in turn, did his best. He drove the ball over the right-field fence. Incredibly, it was his fourth home run of the game!

In the Philadelphia dugout, Earnshaw smiled at his manager and said, "I believe I see now, Mr. Mack. Mahaffey made him hit it to the other field, didn't he?" Connie Mack just shook his head. Lou Gehrig was as tough a hitter as *any* pitcher had ever faced.

Henry Louis Gehrig was born on June 19, 1903, in New York City. His parents, Heinrich and Christina Gehrig, were German immigrants who had come to America in search of a better life. They were hard-working, honest people, but they knew no English when they first arrived in New York. This made it difficult for them to find work, and to take part in the life around them. Mr. Gehrig was trained in Germany as a leaf-hammerer, which meant he could hammer designs into metal sheets. It was a valuable skill, and he earned good wages when there was work for him, but often there were no leaf-hammering jobs to be had. During those bad stretches, Mr. Gehrig earned money as a handyman, a butcher, or a janitor. Sometimes there was leaf-hammering work, but it required him to go to another city. Those months, while he was away in Chicago, Cleveland, or Detroit, were lonely times in the Gehrig house.

Much of the time, Mrs. Gehrig was the family breadwinner. She worked as a cook and housekeeper for wealthy families, and she also made money by doing other people's laundry. In spite of her long hours working for others, Mrs. Gehrig never failed to do her own family's washing, cooking, and sewing.

Before Lou was born, Mrs. Gehrig had given birth to two children, but both of them had died before they were a year old.

When Lou proved to be a healthy baby, Mrs. Gehrig gave him all the love and attention she had saved up for years. She was determined that his life would be better than hers and her husband's, and to accomplish this, Mrs. Gehrig was willing to work day and night.

The devotion of his mother was an important factor in Lou Gehrig's life. When he was a successful baseball player, receiving a high salary, he made sure that his mother and father shared his success. He bought them a fine home, and insisted that they stop working so they could enjoy their old age. It was his way of saying "Thank you!" for all their sacrifices during his childhood.

One of Lou's earliest memories was riding the trolley car with his mother. He wasn't old enough to go to school, so he went with Mrs. Gehrig to her jobs. While she cooked or cleaned house, the boy sat and played quietly in the kitchen. Then, at night, Lou helped his mother carry the laundry she would wash and iron at home.

Those first five years of Lou Gehrig's life did much to form his personality. As an adult, he was shy, quiet, and serious—just like that small boy who was with his mother all day. Lou spent so much time with his mother that he had little chance to make friends. Even on Sunday, when he was free to play in the neighborhood, he was not able to talk to the other children. His parents spoke in German all the time, and that was the language he learned. Not until Lou began attending public school, when he was five years old, did he start to learn English.

School made a big difference in Lou's life in many ways. Once he began to speak English, he made friends. He was still a quiet little boy, but he enjoyed playing with other children. Even before he could speak English well, Lou found a way to communicate with the other boys and girls—through sports.

Lou Gehrig was not a natural athlete, but he was strong, eager to learn, and ready to practice something until he got it right.

When he began playing baseball, soon after he turned five years old, he was a chubby, awkward child. He didn't throw well, catch well, or run the bases well. Still, Lou was always asked to play in the school yard and in street games because he was one of the best hitters in the neighborhood.

For Lou, doing well at baseball was important. He was teased about being clumsy and fat, about not speaking English well, and about his funny clothing. Lou's parents dressed him in the style they knew from Europe, which was different from the American style. When the other children poked fun at him, Lou was too quiet to answer back with words. He let his baseball abilities do the talking for him.

Mr. and Mrs. Gehrig were glad to see their child make friends. They heard Lou talk about baseball all the time, about the bats and balls and gloves the others kids used, and after a while, they realized he didn't have any baseball equipment of his own. Lou never said anything, but it was clear what he wanted. His mother and father set out to make that Christmas of 1908 a special one for Lou.

The Gehrigs were too poor to buy a Christmas tree, but Mr. Gehrig found a small piece of an evergreen. The tree piece lay in the street, waiting for a garbage pickup, when Mr. Gehrig spotted it. He brought it home on Christmas Eve, and hid it in a closet.

After Lou went to bed, the Gehrigs set the little piece of tree on a table and decorated it with walnuts and bits of ribbon. Under the tree they placed Lou's presents, a stocking filled with cookies, nuts, and an orange, and next to the stocking, a baseball glove. It did not cost a lot, but for the Gehrigs it was expensive.

The next morning, when Lou found his presents, he was overjoyed. The glove meant so much to him that it did not matter that it was a right-handed catcher's mitt, and Lou was left-handed. The glove made him a real American baseball player. It was a

Christmas morning he never forgot. When he was grown-up, he said that glove was the best present he ever received.

The winter Lou received his first glove seemed endless to him. Every night, he slept with the glove beside his pillow. He could barely wait until the weather was warm enough for the baseball games to start again. The arrival of spring 1909 was as exciting as any spring he spent in the major leagues.

In Lou's neighborhood, baseball games were played in the morning, before school began. The boys met in a vacant lot or the school yard, as soon as it grew light. Most of the children got up around five o'clock, gulped down breakfast, and raced out to play. The game continued until the school bell called them inside. The children would have played after school, too, but most of them couldn't. As young as they were, Lou and his playmates had jobs or chores to do after school.

It was normal for children to help their families in any way they could. Children might deliver packages, shovel snow, or work in a local store. Even those who did not have paying jobs had responsibilities. Apartments like those where the Gehrigs lived had stoves that burned coal or wood. The fuel for these stoves had to be carried upstairs, and the children were given this task. They also helped with the laundry, cooking, cleaning, taking care of younger brothers and sisters, and anything else that had to be done.

As hard as this life may sound, it could have been worse. At the beginning of the 20th century, it was perfectly legal for children to work full time, for they did not have to attend a single day of school. Lou and his friends knew they were better off than lots of others their age. They might have just a few years of education, but they wouldn't be illiterate.

Mrs. Gehrig wanted more than only a few years of education for Lou. She wanted him to go to high school and to have a good-paying, steady job one day. Mrs. Gehrig dreamed that her son would not be a laborer who did hard, physical work. She pictured him wearing a suit and a starched white shirt, just like the gentlemen for whom she worked as a housekeeper.

Though he was not a fast learner in school, Lou always earned good marks because his mother saw to it that Lou studied. She insisted that he practice his penmanship over and over, so that each letter looked perfect. She made him do arithmetic until there wasn't a single mistake on the page. She showed her love for her son by encouraging him to set high goals and to be a person on whom others could depend.

Lou did not object to his mother's standards, because they were the same standards he set for himself. As an adult, Lou Gehrig did not allow illness, injury, or anything else to keep him out of a baseball game. It was part of his pride and personality to be steady and reliable, as well as a fine ballplayer. Lou Gehrig is best remembered for having played in 2,130 consecutive games—a baseball record until Cal Ripken surpassed it in 1995. This dependability earned Lou the nickname, "The Iron Horse."

Lou's serious attitude began long before he entered the big leagues. He never missed a day of school. Even when he had pneumonia in second grade, he wouldn't stay home. A perfect attendance record was important to him.

At school, Lou did as well in sports as he did in class work. By seventh grade, he was an outstanding shot-putter on the track team. He played running back and tackle on the football team. On the soccer field, he played different positions and enjoyed all of them. But once baseball season began, Lou put all other sports aside.

When Lou was in eighth grade, his father became very ill and could not work. It looked like Lou would have to get a full-time job instead of going on to high school, but Mrs. Gehrig did not want her son to sacrifice his future. Instead, she took a job as cook-housekeeper for a fraternity house at Columbia University.

Mrs. Gehrig's job paid only enough to cover the family's basic

needs, so she continued to take in laundry and to clean other people's houses. Lou helped out, too, by working at the fraternity house on weekends. Then, when Mr. Gehrig was better, he became the janitor of the fraternity house. Because of this work, Lou felt a loyalty to Columbia University. For years before he was a student there, the school meant a lot to him.

In the fall of 1917, Lou entered the High School of Commerce, where he became a baseball star. A schoolmate remembered, "He came to school by subway, took two steps at a time going up and down stairs, seldom wore a vest or topcoat in cold weather, and had a terrific appetite. What made us suddenly realize at Commerce that Lou was different from other varsity ballplayers was a home run that he hit in an intercity game against Lane Tech of Chicago at Wrigley Field."

That Wrigley Field game, which became part of the Lou Gehrig legend, took place on June 28, 1920. Lou had just turned 17, and was about to be graduated from high school. His powerful hitting had carried Commerce High to the New York City championship and earned them the invitation to Chicago, but Lou almost did not get to make the trip.

The teenager had never been outside New York City, and Lou's parents felt he was not ready for an overnight train journey by himself. Besides, they couldn't afford to pay his expenses. The Commerce High coach, Harry Kane, assured the Gehrigs that Lou would be safe. He would watch the boy day and night, he promised. Furthermore, the school was paying for everything. Lou would log thousands of miles on trains during his major-league career, but this was the trip he remembered best.

In the game between Commerce and Lane, Lou's big moment came in the ninth inning. Commerce was ahead, but Lane had its best hitters coming up in the second half of the inning. Commerce, however, had three men on base, and the chance to build a large lead. Gehrig, who hadn't recorded a hit all day, was due to bat. Nervously, he asked Coach Kane, "What should I do?"

With a smile, Kane answered, "Go and hit one out of the park." The way Lou was hitting that day, Kane really did not expect any such thing to happen.

Lou said, "Yes, sir," went to the plate, and swung at the first pitch. The crowd cheered as the ball soared far over the right-field fence. It was a grand-slam homer—a four-run hit blasted with the force of a major leaguer.

The next day, the New York *Daily News* printed Lou's picture, with this line: "Louis Gehrig, Commerce slugger, the New York lad known as the Babe Ruth of the high schools." The Gehrigs were proud of their boy, but even happier when he entered Columbia University. There, he studied engineering, played football, soccer, and, of course, baseball. Lou loved playing sports, but he had no intention of making a career as an athlete. Then trouble came. When Lou finished his sophomore year at Columbia, his father became seriously ill again. This time, his father's illness changed the course of Lou's life.

Lou could not afford to stay in college for his family needed whatever money he could earn. What's more, Mr. Gehrig had to have an operation, and that would be expensive. Lou began to think about becoming a professional baseball player.

Since his high-school days, Lou had been watched by scouts for a number of major-league teams, but whenever they had approached him, he had turned down their offers. Now he let it be known that he was interested in talking to them. As soon as the word got out, the scouts came to see him.

The best offer came from the New York Yankees, who were willing to pay Lou $1,500 for signing a contract. That was a lot of money in those days. It would pay for Mr. Gehrig's operation, and take care of the family while he recuperated. This was what Lou wanted, and he became a Yankee in June 1923. He was 20 years old.

Mr. Gehrig's operation was a success, but Lou's beginning as a major leaguer was not so triumphant. He could hit well, but the rest of his baseball skills needed sharpening. Two years in the minor leagues took care of that, and in 1925, Lou rejoined the Yankees. From June 1 of that year until May 2, 1939, Lou Gehrig never missed playing in a game. During those 14 seasons with the Yankees, he became one of America's sports idols. Along with Babe Ruth, Gehrig led the New York Yankees through their Golden Era. In fact, the Yankees of 1927 are called by many, "the greatest team in baseball history."

Lou set many records in his career. He hit a record total of 23 grand-slam home runs. He led the American League four times in runs scored, five times in home runs, and was voted the league's Most Valuable Player four times. He was one of the greatest hitters of all time.

By 1938, baseball's "Iron Horse" was beginning to slow down. Some days his hitting was as superb as ever, yet on other days he could barely hit the ball. At first, he ignored these batting slumps, but after a while, it was clear that something was wrong.

Gehrig started the 1939 season with the hope that he would be back in top form, but he was worse than ever. A medical examination showed the reason. Lou had a disease that slowly destroys the nervous system. He was told he had a short time to live, and that the condition could not be cured.

When Lou Gehrig retired from baseball in May 1939, the sports world was stunned. It did not seem possible that this strong young man, who looked as if he could play forever, was dying. Sadly, it was true, and people rushed to show their respect and admiration. Lou did not have to wait to be voted into the Baseball Hall of Fame. The waiting rule was set aside, and he was unanimously voted in that same year.

On July 4, 1939, the Yankees retired his uniform, Number 4, forever. The ceremonies took place at Yankee Stadium, on Lou

Gehrig Appreciation Day. Between the first and second games of a double-header, a microphone was set up at home plate. Many people paid tribute to Lou Gehrig, the man called the "Pride of the Yankees." There was his old teammate, Babe Ruth; New York City's Mayor Fiorello LaGuardia; players from the past and present; sportswriters; and baseball officials.

Then, as more than 70,000 people listened, Lou Gehrig said with deep feeling, "Fans, for the past two weeks you have been reading about a bad break I got. Yet today I consider myself the luckiest man on the face of the earth. I have been in ballparks for 17 years, and have never received anything but kindness and encouragement from you fans. . . . So I close in saying that I might have had a tough break; but I have an awful lot to live for."

Two years later, on June 2, 1941, Lou Gehrig died. It was exactly 16 years from the day he began his unbroken streak of consecutive baseball games. 'The Iron Horse" was now a part of sports history.

Jackie Robinson

The pitcher reared back and threw. The baseball whizzed toward home plate, but it wasn't heading anywhere near the catcher's mitt. It was aimed directly at the head of the batter, Jackie Robinson. Jackie jumped out of the way and went sprawling in the dirt. Then he stood right back up and got ready for the next pitch. It curved over the plate, and Robinson doubled sharply down the left-field line. The crowd cheered, and his teammates joined in.

The year was 1947. Jackie Robinson, first baseman for the Brooklyn Dodgers, was the first and only black player in the major leagues, and the target of hate and bigotry in and out of the sport. Hotels closed their doors to him. Fans at every rival ballpark screamed ugly words at him. Even some of his own teammates were cruel to him. Worst of all, certain pitchers always threw at his head. Still, Jackie never backed down.

He had a cool explanation for standing his ground, saying it was part of his strategy. "After you have ducked away from a close one, you can expect a curve ball." And he jumped on those curve balls every time.

But there was more to it than that. Robinson wasn't just

using his brains to get base hits, he was also showing great courage. A 95-mile-an-hour fastball is terrifying when it's coming right at you, but Robinson wasn't about to let anyone drive him away from the major leagues because of the color of his skin. He wasn't going to be defeated!

In the early years of the 20th century, life was very hard for African Americans all over the United States, but especially in the southern states. It was more than 50 years after the end of the Civil War, yet black people still suffered terrible discrimination.

Mallie and Jerry Robinson lived in a wooden shack near Cairo, Georgia. They were not slaves as their parents had been, but their lives were hardly any better. They lived in a house owned by a white farmer named Jim Sasser and farmed a section of his land. They paid Sasser for the land they worked and the house they lived in out of the profit they made when they sold their crops. Besides that, the Robinsons had to buy whatever they needed from Sasser. The seeds they planted, the feed they gave their chickens, their clothing, tools, and anything else they needed came from Sasser's general store. By the time they paid Sasser for everything, there was little left for the Robinsons.

Every year was a 365-day struggle for Mallie and Jerry Robinson, but worst of all, it was a life without hope. The laws of Georgia said they could not own land. There were separate schools for blacks—schools without books, without heat, sometimes without trained teachers. African Americans had no civil rights, and they were not allowed to vote. The Robinsons may not have been slaves, but they were not free in any real way.

On the evening of January 31, 1919, the Robinsons' fifth child was born. They named him Jack Roosevelt Robinson. He had three brothers—Edgar, Frank, and Mack—and a sister named Willa Mae. Jackie was a bright-eyed, strong baby, and a joy to his parents, but he was also another mouth to feed in a household that was already on the edge of starvation.

The strain of trying to survive became too much for Mr. Robinson to handle. He left, never to return. Mrs. Robinson knew she and the children had to leave the farm soon. At that time, Mrs. Robinson's brother, Frank, came to visit. After learning what had happened, he said, "Georgia is no place for your kids. Come out to California. Things are better there. You'll have me and you'll have other kinfolk, too. It's a chance for a better life. You owe it to that happy little baby. Give Jackie a better world to grow up in. Give him a chance to become somebody."

To Mrs. Robinson, Georgia was home, and the thought of leaving frightened her. Only the promise of a real future for her children gave her the courage she needed. Over the next six months Mrs. Robinson did everything necessary to make the long trip. She sold the chickens, her few pieces of furniture, and every bit of clothing the family could spare. She even sold her pots, pans, and dishes. Every penny went into a jar marked California.

By the spring of 1920, the Robinsons had enough money to pay for the train tickets to California. The cross-country trip took almost a week in a section of the train marked "COLORED ONLY." The seats were wooden, and sitting on them day after day and night after night hurt a lot.

Mrs. Robinson had no money to buy food during the trip. On the day before they left Georgia, she packed sandwiches and some cakes. "We have to make this food last," she told her children. "There will be no more till we get to California. So we'll do the best we can and not make a fuss about anything."

It was a long trip across the country, but finally the Robinsons were met by relatives at the railroad station in Pasadena, California. Along with Frank were Mrs. Robinson's half-brother, Burton McGriff, and his wife, Mary Lou. It was wonderful to get off the train at last, and to see smiling, friendly faces. Mrs. Robinson had faith that this was the beginning of a better life for all of them.

The McGriffs lived in an apartment with three rooms and a kitchen. Even before the Robinsons arrived, the apartment was crowded. The McGriffs already had four children and a cousin living with them. With the Robinsons, there were 13 people squeezed into those three rooms.

The crowded apartment had other problems. There was no hot water, and the tin tub in the kitchen used for washing dishes was also used for bathing. Since there was no electricity, an old-fashioned oil lamp was the only source of light besides sunshine. Food was cooked on a wood-burning stove.

At first, cooking wasn't a problem for the Robinsons. They had no money to buy food. The children's diet was mainly stale bread the local baker gave to them, and water mixed with sugar. The McGriffs offered to share their food, but Mrs. Robinson was too proud to accept.

Things got a little better when she found work as a domestic servant, cleaning houses, and washing and ironing clothing for families in Pasadena. Mrs. Robinson didn't earn much money, but the work had other benefits. The clothing outgrown by children of these families was sometimes passed on to the Robinson youngsters.

As Jackie Robinson later wrote, "Sometimes there were only two meals a day, and some days we wouldn't have eaten at all if it hadn't been for the leftovers my mother was able to bring home from her jobs."

Mrs. Robinson had her own system of child care. Each of her children was responsible for the next younger child. Only Jackie, the youngest, was not expected to look after anyone else. Despite all their problems, the Robinsons were a close, loving family. The children stood up for each other, and the bigger ones protected the smaller ones. Jackie, the baby of the house, was surrounded by love and protection.

Mrs. Robinson was grateful to the McGriffs for taking in her family, but she felt it was unfair to take too much from them. She saved every penny possible, and at last, with her small savings and help from the Pasadena Welfare Department, Mrs. Robinson was able to buy a house.

The Robinsons' new home wasn't grand, but it was large enough, and there was a front porch and a small yard. There was a back yard, too, with room to play and grow a vegetable garden. On moving day, Mrs. Robinson sang as the children chased each other upstairs and downstairs through the rooms. Jackie, who was still a toddler, giggled and tried to keep up with everybody.

There was just one thing wrong. The neighbors didn't like having a black family living among them, and these bad feelings lasted many years. One incident burned itself into Jackie's memory forever. When he was eight years old, his mother sent him out to sweep the sidewalk. A little girl across the street started shouting, "Nigger, nigger, nigger!"

Jackie was hurt. He shouted back, "You're nothing but a cracker!" He thought that was a very insulting word to say to a white person.

The little girl's father rushed out of the house, picked up a stone, and threw it at Jackie. Jackie dropped his broom, picked up the stone, and threw it back at the man. The stone-throwing went on for a few minutes until finally the girl's mother came out and pulled her husband inside. Jackie heard her say it was crazy for a grown man to get into a fight with a child.

As an African American, Mrs. Robinson faced bigotry all the time. It hurt her deeply, but she refused to lower herself to the level of her attackers. As an adult, Jackie Robinson wrote, "My mother taught us to respect ourselves and to demand respect from others. . . . My mother never lost her composure. She didn't allow us to go out of our way to antagonize the whites, and she still made it perfectly clear to us and to them that she was not at all afraid of them and that she had no intention of allowing them to mistreat us."

Jackie learned another important lesson as a child, and that was to take care of himself. When Willa Mae entered kindergarten at the Grover Cleveland School, there was nobody at home to take care of little Jackie, so Mrs. Robinson sent Jackie to school with his sister. Miss Haney, the teacher, objected and sent a note home to Mrs. Robinson, saying Jackie must not come to school with Willa Mae.

The next morning, Mrs. Robinson went to see Miss Haney. "If I have to stay home to watch Jackie, I can't work," Mrs. Robinson said. "If I can't work, we'll have to go on welfare. I have too much pride to do that. I want to work!" Then Mrs. Robinson asked that Jackie be allowed to play in the sandbox right outside the classroom. "He's a mighty good boy," she said. "He'll play there without bothering anyone."

Miss Haney admired Mrs. Robinson's pride and determination, and she agreed to the unusual request. Every day the little boy sat in the sandbox and played all by himself. Sometimes Jackie was lonely, but he knew that it was important for him to be very good and to be quiet.

One morning it started to rain. When Miss Haney looked out the window and saw Jackie sitting in the sandbox, his shirt was soaking wet, but he was not complaining or crying. The teacher hurried outside, took the little boy by the hand, and led him into the classroom. Jackie behaved so well that Miss Haney praised him and asked Willa Mae to tell her mother what a wonderful child he was. From then on, Jackie was invited inside anytime it rained. He was also included whenever the class had a party.

Jackie's behavior was the first sign that he had a special strength. Somehow Jackie Robinson was able to deal with a tough situation and come out a winner. He won the respect of Miss Haney and the whole class, and he helped his mother solve a real problem.

Jackie felt lucky to have Miss Haney as his own teacher when he entered kindergarten. He never forgot her. "She judged me as an individual," he wrote many years later, "and not by the color of my skin. She inspired me to believe that my chances for equal treatment from others were as good as anyone else's, provided that I applied myself to the task at hand."

Young Jackie was a hard-working student and he got good grades, but his finest efforts were at sports. While he was at Grover Cleveland School, Jackie recalled, "I told my mother to save money by not fixing lunch for me. The other kids brought me sandwiches and dimes for the movies so they could play on my team. You might say I turned pro at an early age.

"I discovered that in one sector of life in southern California I was free to compete with whites on equal terms—in sports. I played soccer on my fourth-grade team against sixth-graders who were two or three years older than I. Soon I was competing in other sports against opponents of every size, shape, and color. . . . The more I played the better I became—in softball, hardball, football, basketball, tennis, table tennis, any kind of game with a ball. I played hard and always to win!"

A close childhood friend remembered Jackie's speed and concentration. One of the games they played was dodge ball. A dodge-ball game has two teams, one of which forms a wide circle around the other. Players on the outside team try to hit players on the inside team with a large ball, while players on the inside team dodge this way and that to avoid being hit. When a player is hit, he is out of the game. The winner is the last kid inside the circle. When Jackie was on the inside team, he was always the winner. As his friend said, "The game finally had to stop because nobody could hit Jackie."

Jackie had more than natural athletic ability going for him.

Edgar, Frank, Mack, and Willa Mae were also fine athletes, and they all loved to coach their younger brother. The Robinsons were the most athletic family in the neighborhood. They played football, baseball, soccer, and field hockey, and at school they all ran track.

Jackie always played with the big kids, and his brother, Mack, felt this did Jackie a lot of good. The youngest Robinson wasn't as large or as strong as his older teammates, but he was fast and smart. He had to be to get into their games.

When Jackie Robinson grew up he became a star with the Brooklyn Dodgers. His speed and quick reflexes on the base paths made him one of the best base-runners in the major leagues. He averaged 20 stolen bases a year over his career. No pitcher relaxed when Jackie was on base.

Young Jackie went from Grover Cleveland School to George Washington Junior High School and then to Muir Technical High School. Wherever he went, he was the No. 1 athlete. In high school he won letters in baseball, football, track, and basketball. Jackie's greatness was known all over Pasadena.

Before every game against Muir—in any sport—the other team's battle cry was "Stop Robinson!" but as hard as they tried, they couldn't. Some opponents tried to knock him out of the game physically, while others tried insulting him. Jackie was called things that demeaned his race, his family, anything that might hurt him. The players wanted to get him angry enough so that he would lose his concentration and control. Jackie knew what they were trying to do, and he closed his ears to everything they said.

Jackie was still in high school in 1936 when the name of Robinson became known around the world, but it wasn't Jackie who became famous—it was his big brother Mack. Jackie's brother was a member of the United States Olympic track team. Mack won a silver medal in the 200-meter dash in Berlin,

Germany, losing the gold to his legendary teammate, Jesse Owens.

Jackie was really proud of his brother. Mack was a winner, and Jackie vowed he was going to be one, too. Pasadena Junior College wasn't known as a sports powerhouse until the Robinsons arrived. First there was Mack, then came Jackie. Between them they put the school on the national sports pages.

In 1939, Jackie finished junior college and entered the University of California at Los Angeles. He planned to become a high school teacher and a coach after graduation. Although he was an athletic superstar at UCLA, Jackie never considered becoming a professional athlete. In those days, blacks were not welcome in the major leagues in any sport.

Jackie Robinson didn't graduate from UCLA, leaving during his senior year. Mrs. Robinson needed his help with the family expenses, and that was good enough reason for him to leave behind the cheers of the fans for a full-time job. Soon after that, World War II began, and Jackie entered the U.S. Army. In time he became Lieutenant Robinson and was made morale officer for an African-American unit.

After his discharge, in November, 1944, Jackie had to decide what to do with his life. He was offered a job as basketball coach at Sam Houston College, an all-black school in Texas, and he was about to take it when, in April 1945, he received an offer to play shortstop with the Kansas City Monarchs of the Negro Leagues.

In those days, there were separate leagues for black and white baseball players. The Monarchs were one of the best teams in the Negro Leagues. Jackie took the job, which paid $400 a month. That wasn't much money, but it was a chance to play baseball—and get paid for it.

That same year, Jackie Robinson met Branch Rickey, the general manager of the Brooklyn Dodgers, and the two men got along very well. It was a meeting that changed Jackie's life and the history of American sports. Branch Rickey had a daring dream: to wipe out racism in baseball. The first step to make that dream come true was to hire an exceptional black player. That great player had to have the strength not to fall apart or lose his temper when bigoted fans and players insulted him. It didn't take long for Rickey to see that Jackie Robinson was that man.

On October 23, 1945, Jackie Robinson signed a contract with the Brooklyn Dodgers organization. Rickey assigned him to the Montreal Royals, one step below the major leagues. Jackie played second base for the Royals in 1946, and led the league that season in batting, with a .349 average, fielding, with a .985 average, and scoring, with 113 runs. He also stole 40 bases. But even more important, he led the league in self-control. Branch Rickey knew Jackie was ready to take the next big step.

On April 10, 1947, the newspaper carried this announcement: "The Brooklyn Dodgers today purchased the contract of Jack Roosevelt Robinson, from the Montreal Royals. He will report immediately."

For the next 10 years, Jackie Robinson starred for the Brooklyn Dodgers. His first season was tough, and a few of his Dodger teammates refused to play with him. Players on other teams tried to spike him, and some pitchers threw fastballs at his head, but Number 42 refused to break. He answered back by playing baseball the best he could, and his best was great!

Jackie Robinson's baseball statistics are outstanding. His career batting average was .311. He led the National League in stolen bases in 1947 and 1949. Playing second base, he was voted Most Valuable Player in 1949, when he led the league in batting. Jackie retired in 1956, and in 1962 he was inducted into baseball's Hall of Fame.

By 1972, when Jackie Robinson died, it was not unusual to see a black player in a major-league uniform, and today African-

American professionals excel in every sport. But Jackie Robinson's legacy is even more valuable than that, for his bravery and pride changed the way African Americans are treated in and out of sports. Most important, it changed the way many blacks look at themselves. As the great Martin Luther King, Jr. said, "You will never know how easy it was for me because of Jackie Robinson."

Willie Mays

Baseball history is filled with the names of great athletes and champions, but nobody ever played the game with more joy, style, and genuine ability than Willie Mays. He was a fan's dream come true. Willie Mays could do it all. He hit—and hit with power. He ran with the speed and grace of a greyhound. He threw with strength and accuracy. He chased down and caught hit balls that other fielders might have given up on. Willie was a "natural," an athlete with amazing ability, whom many people think was the greatest ballplayer who ever lived.

Willie was born on May 6, 1931, in Westfield, Alabama. Both of his parents were 18 years old and just out of high school. Willie's mother, Ann, was a high-school track star who had set a number of records as a runner in Westfield. His father, William Howard Mays, was a fine outfielder in Birmingham, Alabama's Industrial League. Sports played a big part in Willie's life from his very first days.

At the time Willie was born, his father was working in a steel mill at a low paying job. The doors of opportunity were often shut for black people in those days, but Mr. Mays wanted his son to have a better life than he had. Playing sports for a living seemed to be the best answer. Mr. Mays had dreamed of being a star baseball player himself, but marriage and fatherhood made that almost impossible, so he dreamed the good life for his son.

Willie Mays was an active baby. He took his first steps when he was just six months old. Right away, his father introduced him to sports. "As soon as he started walking," Willie's father recalled, "I bought him a big round ball. He'd hold that ball and then he'd bounce it and chase it. And if he ever couldn't get that ball, he'd cry."

Willie Mays and a ball—it was a perfect combination. Mr. Mays put a baseball on one chair. He put another chair a couple of feet away. Then he stood little Willie by the second chair. "See the ball?" his father asked. "Can you get it?" The baby smiled and toddled to the ball. He grabbed it in both hands, laughing happily. "Great!" Mr. Mays cried. "Now, give Daddy the ball."

They played this game over and over, and each time, Mr. Mays moved the chairs a little farther apart. Soon, baby Willie was toddling across the entire room to get the ball. That was Willie Mays' first fielding lesson in baseball.

Batting lessons came next. Mr. Mays sat Willie in the middle of the floor. He gave the baby a stick about two feet long, then he sat down and rolled the ball to his son. "Can you hit the ball?" Mr. Mays asked. "Come on, hit the ball to Daddy."

Little Willie giggled. A ball and a stick were his favorite toys. He spent hours playing with the ball. He hit it with the stick, then he chased it across the room and hit it again. Willie never grew tired of this simple game. Even when he went to sleep, he kept the ball and stick next to him.

When Willie Mays was three years old, his parents were divorced. Mr. Mays adored his bright-eyed little boy and wanted Willie with him, but that left Mr. Mays with a problem. For a year, Mr. Mays had been working at a different, better-paying job with the railroad. He took care of passengers' luggage on a train that went back and forth between Birmingham, Alabama, and Detroit, Michigan. Mr. Mays hoped to save enough money to buy something special—his own home in a nice neighborhood. He wanted his son to grow up in a warm, comfortable house, so he saved every nickel he could for that house he wanted so much.

But his railroad job often kept him away from home, so Mr. Mays needed someone to look after his little boy. When a neighbor died, leaving two daughters who needed a home, Mr. Mays took them in.

The teenage girls were named Sarah and Ernestine. All at once, Willie had a family. Sarah and Ernestine were like mothers and sisters and good friends to the three-year-old boy. When Daddy was away, they made sure Willie was clean and fed and safe. This was a great help to Mr. Mays. It was a wonderful arrangement for the girls, too. Mr. Mays' kindness kept them from being homeless, so they were just as happy to be a part of Mr. Mays' family as he was to have them. Willie loved the girls, whom he called Aunt Sarah and Aunt Ernestine.

Mr. Mays missed Willie very much when he was away on train trips, so even though the steel-mill job paid less money, Mr. Mays went back to work there. He was glad to be with his little boy again, but he was a little sad that he had to put off the dream of owning his own home.

The Westfield house Mr. Mays lived in and paid rent for was owned by the steel company. In fact, the company owned most of the land and businesses in Westfield, Alabama. Westfield was a company town. Workers at the mill were not paid in money, but in company chips each Friday. When a mill worker needed new clothing, he bought it at one of the company stores in the mill. When a worker needed food, he bought it at another company store.

The steel company had great control over its workers. It paid only in chips, and only company stores accepted chips as payment. So the workers were forced to buy everything from the company.

The money Mr. Mays had earned while working for the railroad was put into a bank account, and he added to it by doing part-time work that paid real money, not chips. He also played baseball for a semiprofessional team. The pay wasn't much, but every penny of it went into Mr. Mays' "dream house" bank account. Ernestine, a waitress in a local restaurant, also contributed to the family income.

Ernestine gave Willie money each week so he could buy lunch at school. Since there was no school cafeteria, Willie and his friends went to a nearby grocery store. He bought bread, lunch meat, fruit, cake, and milk. Then the children went to an empty lot and shared the food. In the evening, Willie often brought friends home for dinner, and Sarah would feed them all.

Willie Mays didn't know that his family was poor. The house was comfortable, there was enough food to eat, and Willie was encouraged to share his lunch money and to invite friends home for dinner. As poor as Willie's family was, his friends' families were even poorer.

Willie was growing up in the 1930s, the time of the Great Depression. Millions of Americans were out of work, and there was hunger and homelessness in every part of the country. Willie was lucky that his father and Ernestine had jobs, and that Sarah was a good homemaker who saw to it that every dollar went a long way.

Willie was surrounded by kindness and love. Without ever making a big thing of it, the Mays family gave true meaning to the word "charity." Willie came to understand this when he was a grown man.

Even as a child, Willie's world was centered around baseball. He was good, right from the start, and when he rushed out of school every day, he was ready to play. The vacant lot where Willie and his friends ate lunch became a ball field in the afternoon. They played with the barest of equipment. They had no uniforms, no special shoes or spikes, no catcher's mask or chest protector, and no batting helmet. Most of the children didn't even own a glove. They used a stick as a bat and played with whatever ball was available. They just chose up sides and played for the fun of it.

When it was time to choose sides, Willie was one of the first picked. Sometimes, older children played on the lot. Even then, Willie was welcome as a player. He could run, throw, slide, hit, and catch the ball as well as any boy in town.

Willie's eyesight was better than normal. He could look straight ahead and see things that were happening in front and on both sides of him. Many great athletes have this wide range of vision, which helps them to see everything going on in the game. This is true in baseball, basketball, football, and many other sports.

Willie also had very large hands. "I knew he'd be a good ballplayer," Mr. Mays remembered. "It's those big hands of his. With hands that big, he never had trouble catching the ball." Willie did have big hands for his age, but he also had great timing and speed. Most of all, he worked at learning to catch well. Whenever Mr. Mays had a moment to spare, he played ball with his son. They started when Willie was five years old. Father and son had a special game that they played for hours at a time. Mr. Mays bounced the ball to Willie, and the boy caught it after one bounce and threw it back. It was like the game they played when Willie was just learning to walk.

Mr. Mays did something even more special. When he went to play in Industrial League games, he took Willie with him. The boy was allowed to sit on the bench with the grown-up players. It was a thrill for Willie, and it was fun for Mr. Mays, too. There was another advantage to having Willie in the dugout—the whole team acted as baby sitters while Mr. Mays was playing.

Willie got much more than fun out of those days. The players in the dugout talked about batting against different kinds of pitchers. They talked about stealing bases and about how to play on wet or very rough fields. They talked about bunting, and how to catch a ball cleanly and then throw it quickly to the right base. Everything it took to play the game well was discussed in that dugout. Willie listened because it was so interesting, not realizing that he was getting a priceless education in the sport.

Before the games, the players stayed in the locker room, and Willie was free to run all over the field. He made believe he was his father stealing second base . . . third base . . . home. He slid hard into each bag. He loved running and sliding into one base after another. After all this sliding, Willie's clothes were very dirty; after every game Sarah jokingly complained about how filthy Willie got while his father was playing.

Mr. Mays was an excellent outfielder who could run down balls hit anywhere in his part of the outfield. His ability to make amazing catches and throws and to pounce on a hit ball with speed and smoothness earned him the nicknames "Kitty-Kat" and "Cat." Willie worked hard to be just like his father, and this made Mr. Mays happy. He hoped his son would be a professional baseball player, but he did not push Willie. Baseball had to be something Willie wanted, and right from the start Willie certainly wanted to play the game. His love of baseball grew even stronger when he learned that his father was paid to play. "That seemed to me," Willie Mays remembered, "just about the nicest idea anyone ever thought up."

To Willie Mays, both as a child and as an adult, the sport was pure joy, and the fans could feel Willie's delight. It was in the way he ran, taking swift, sure strides. It was in how he raced around the bases. It was in dozens of unforgettable catches and throws. It was in the ball-crushing swing of his bat. It was in his wide grin and the way his hat flew off as he ran to catch a ball or take an extra base. And it was in the way he said "Say hey!" to express his pleasure at one thing or another. Willie Mays simply loved the game!

Young Willie also enjoyed other sports. Like many boys, he played whatever sport was in season. In the fall, it was football. In the winter, it was both football and basketball, but best of all was baseball, which he played in the spring, summer, and fall.

When Willie was 10 years old, the family finally moved into the "dream house" Mr. Mays always wanted. It was a neat cottage in a Birmingham suburb called Fairfield. There was a grassy lawn, a big front porch, and a nice back yard. It wasn't a large house, but Mr. Mays owned it. At last, he didn't have to pay rent for a company house.

Willie liked his new neighborhood and his new school. Soon, he made friends with Charlie Willis, a boy who lived a few houses away. Willie and Charlie became best friends, and they stayed best friends from then on. The boys were both crazy about sports, movies, and comic books. They walked to school together, throwing a ball back and forth. They shared comic books, went to the movies together regularly, and listened to the radio together. If Charlie and Willie weren't playing ball outside, they were in each other's house. The boys were as close as brothers.

Willie called Charlie "Cool," and Charlie called Willie "Buck." These nicknames stuck with them even as grown-ups, but Willie the professional ballplayer was never called Buck by his teammates. It was a name used only by people who knew him as a boy in Birmingham, Alabama.

When Willie was about 12 years old, he fell out of a tree and broke his right arm. At first, Willie didn't know his arm was broken, and he rushed home, paying no attention to the pain. He was more upset about falling and looking silly. He was also worried about being punished for climbing a tree, for that was something his father had told him not to do. When the pain got worse, Willie could no longer hide it, so he told his father everything. Mr. Mays didn't punish Willie. He just made sure the doctor took care of his arm.

When Willie's arm was healed, it was very strong. Before the break, he threw underhand, and while those throws were good, they were not great. After the arm healed, Willie was more comfortable throwing overhand, and his throws were faster, stronger, and more accurate than ever.

One day, while Willie was playing baseball with his friends, he was asked to play with the Gray Sox, a semiprofessional team in Fairfield. All the other players were at least two years older than the 13-year-old Mays boy, and Willie was quick to say yes.

At first, Willie played shortstop, but that didn't last long. His excitement got the better of him, and every time he fielded the ball, he threw it to first base as hard as he could. It was so hard that the first baseman complained.

"Willie," the manager said, "I think your arm's too good to waste at shortstop. I want you to pitch our next game."

Willie was thrilled at the idea. The pitcher was the star—the game was in his hands. The crowd cheered Willie as he pitched the Gray Sox's next game and became an instant star. His fastball was too much for the other team to hit. After the game, Willie couldn't wait to get home and tell his father about his fantastic pitching. Mr. Mays listened silently, and when Willie was finished, his father praised him. Then Mr. Mays asked Willie not to pitch another game. Willie didn't understand until his father explained why.

"If a pitcher hurts his arm," Mr. Mays said, "he's finished in baseball . . . unless he knows how to play the *whole* game. Now, most pitchers never bother to learn anything but pitching. I don't want that to happen to you. You've got to work on hitting, fielding, throwing—everything. Maybe you will be a pitcher someday, maybe not. But whatever you are, you'll be a complete ballplayer. I don't want you to waste your whole future by trying to be a star at 13."

Willie was disappointed, but he obeyed his father. He knew Mr. Mays was really wise when it came to baseball. The boy worked on improving his all-around game and left pitching to other players on the team. His father proved to be right, and Willie had a long career. He reached the major leagues in 1951 and played for 23 years.

During the summers of 1945 and 1946, Willie played in the Industrial League with his father. Mr. Mays was in center field, and Willie was in left field. The teenager was getting better every game, while the father was getting a little slower every game. Near the end of the 1946 season, something happened that Willie never forgot. A ball was hit into left-center field. Mr. Mays called out, "I'll take it!" When Willie saw that his father would not get to the ball in time, he cut in front of his father and gloved the ball just before it hit the ground.

Willie and his father never talked about that moment, but Mr. Mays stopped playing baseball after the 1946 summer season ended. He felt sad for himself but very proud of his son. He showed his pride by taking Willie to meet Piper Davis, manager of the Birmingham Black Barons. They were one of the top teams in the Negro Leagues, and Mr. Mays wanted Davis to give Willie a tryout for the Black Barons.

At the time, the Negro Leagues were the only place in the U.S. where African American athletes could play pro baseball. Although they were not allowed in the major leagues, the black players on the black teams were just as good as those in the major leagues. That became clear in 1947, the year former Negro League star Jackie Robinson became the first African American player in the major leagues. As a member of the Brooklyn Dodgers, Jackie was an instant major-league star. He was soon followed by other fine players from the Negro Leagues. Among them were Hank Aaron, Roy Campanella, Larry Doby, Monte Irvin, and Satchel Paige.

When Willie Mays was growing up, he never imagined himself playing in the major leagues. His dream was to play for the Black Barons, so he was thrilled to be given a tryout by Piper Davis.

Willie did well at his tryout and was invited to join the team. That's when Mr. Mays set down the rules: Willie had to get good grades and finish high school; he was allowed to play on weekends and during summer vacations; if Willie's grades slipped, it meant no baseball. Even if Willie didn't like the rules, he had to accept them. He was too young to sign a contract for himself, and besides, Willie knew that his father had his best interests at heart.

There was someone else looking after Willie's best interests. He was E. T. Oliver, the principal of Fairfield Industrial High School. Mr. Oliver kept a close eye on Willie, and made sure Willie gave full attention to his schoolwork. Mr. Oliver really cared about his students and had strict but fair rules. "Get educated," he told the students, and they knew he meant it. Mr. Oliver felt that good grades and good behavior came *before* sports and social life.

Willie Mays always remembered Mr. Oliver with respect, and he was proud and pleased to say he was a high-school graduate. Many major leaguers today go to college, but when Willie was playing, most ballplayers did not finish high school. That might not have hurt them while they were playing ball, but it did once they were finished, because they did not have the skills and education for a new career.

With high school behind him, Willie became a full-time player with the Black Barons. Now that the major leagues were open to African American ballplayers, the scouts were keeping a close watch on Willie, and they saw him hit over .300 for the 1948 and 1949 seasons. His hitting and fielding made him a first-rate prospect, and in the middle of the 1950 season, Willie Mays was signed by the New York Giants of the National League. They gave him a small amount of money for signing, then sent him to New Jersey to play for the Trenton Giants. It was a Class B minor-league team.

Willie remembered that time clearly. "I realized I was a pioneer," he said. "Not only was I the first black player on the Trenton Giants, I was the first in the entire league."

Mays was sensational with Trenton, and the next year, he was moved up to the Minneapolis Millers. The Millers were a Triple-A team in the American Association. That meant the 19-year-old superstar was one step from the major leagues. After 35 games at Minneapolis, Willie was batting a league-leading .477! At that point, he was brought up to the New York Giants. Willie Mays was a major leaguer at last!

When he didn't get a hit in the first few games he played, he was ashamed and ready to quit, but Manager Leo Durocher wouldn't let him. "As long as I'm manager of the Giants," Durocher told him, "you're my center fielder. You're here to stay. Stop worrying. With your talent, you're going to get plenty of hits."

Mays did just that, helping the Giants win the 1951 National League pennant in an exciting race with the Brooklyn Dodgers. He won Rookie of the Year honors that year, but perhaps most important of all, he won the hearts of baseball fans everywhere. It was a love affair that lasted his entire career.

Willie started his major-league career with the Giants in New York. When the team moved to San Francisco, he continued to be a Giant star, then, to the joy of New Yorkers, he returned to join the New York Mets in 1972. Willie played two seasons with the Mets, helping them win the National League pennant in 1973. After that, he retired.

During his career, Willie Mays slugged 660 home runs. Only Hank Aaron and Babe Ruth ever hit more. Twice, Willie hit 50 or more homers in a single season. In 1954, he showed what a complete hitter he was by winning the National League batting title. At one time or another, he also led the National League in triples, runs, hits, stolen bases, and bases on balls, and he played great defense in the outfield. It came as no surprise to anyone when Willie was elected to the Baseball Hall of Fame in 1979. It was the first year he was eligible, and he was voted in on the first ballot.

For millions of fans, Willie Mays *was* baseball. He was a brilliant hitter, base runner, and fielder, and his bubbly personality won him friends and admirers everywhere. No player ever gave more to the game than Willie Mays. He was truly a fan's dream come true.

Roberto Clemente

The Pittsburgh Pirates were ahead by a score of 1–0 in the top of the seventh inning, but that wasn't much of a lead against a hard-hitting team like the San Francisco Giants, and now the Giants' best hitter was up at bat. The Pirate pitcher whipped a fastball toward the plate. The batter swung and connected, sending the ball bulleting toward the right-field wall.

At the *crack!* of bat against ball, the right fielder, Roberto Clemente, whirled and raced toward the wall. Clemente's left arm reached up and the ball smacked into his glove. Then Clemente himself slammed into the concrete wall, and blood spurted from his cut chin.

Clemente fell to his knees, stunned. He shook his head to clear it, then he raised the glove, showing the white ball nestled in the brown leather pocket. The crowd went wild. "Arriba! Arriba!" thousands of Pittsburgh fans screamed. The jubilant cry followed him every step of the way back to the Pirate dugout.

"Arriba!" was the hometown fans' way of telling Roberto Clemente just how much they loved him. By cheering him in Spanish, the fans were saying something special to the great Puerto Rican-born ballplayer.

For Roberto Clemente, the hometown fans' approval was very important. Baseball was his life, and he wanted to be a perfect player every inning of every game. He was proud when he did well, and he felt very happy when his fans appreciated what he was doing for them.

Pride and hard work were a big part of Roberto Clemente, and they were also the source of his family's strength. Hard work was a Clemente tradition. For as long as they could remember, the family was admired for doing a job well.

Melchor and Luisa Clemente lived in the Barrio San Anton, in Carolina, a town in Puerto Rico. Carolina, part of the countryside in those days, is about ten miles from San Juan, the capital of this lovely Caribbean island. When Roberto Clemente was a boy, the Barrio San Anton had tiny, twisting streets dotted with small, modest houses. Everyone in the barrio was poor, but the district was not a slum. Like the rest of the people of Carolina, its residents were hard-working laborers and shopkeepers.

Sugar cane provided the main source of employment for Carolina's citizens. They labored in the fields, planting, cutting, and gathering the cane. They loaded and drove the wagons that carried the cane to processing plants, and they worked in the plants, turning the crop into sugar to be shipped all over the world.

Melchor Clemente, Roberto's father, was in charge of a crew of cane-cutters. It was his job to see that the men worked well and earned their pay. He also made sure that the crew was treated fairly by the sugar company's management.

Melchor was a quiet, thoughtful, even-tempered man. The workers respected him, and so did his family. "Honor comes from what you are, not what you possess," Mr. Clemente often said. His rules for living were firm: you paid back any money you owed, you kept your dignity, and you contributed to the well-being of your family. You also helped others less fortunate than yourself.

Luisa Clemente, Roberto's mother, also set high standards.

She was deeply religious, warmhearted, and devoted to her family. Together, Luisa and Melchor were wonderful parents to their children, two of whom, Luis and Rosa Maria Oquendo, were Luisa's children from her first marriage. Their father died when they were still toddlers, but Melchor Clemente treated them as his own. The Clementes also had five boys: Oswaldo, Justino, Andres, Martino, and Roberto.

Roberto, the youngest, was born at home on August 18, 1934. He was a strong, healthy, handsome baby, the pet of the family. His brother, Martino, remembered Roberto's childhood clearly. "Basically, Roberto was a good kid. He did two things, played ball and stayed home. He never got into trouble. He was always quiet, never got spanked. We used to kid him about that."

The family's nickname for Roberto was Mome (pronounced Mo-may). Nobody recalled how he got the name. The word didn't mean anything, but it caught on. Soon everyone called him Mome. Roberto liked it, so he used that name when he started school.

The Clemente home was comfortable and roomy enough for the large family. There was a living room, dining room, kitchen, five bedrooms, and a shady front porch. There was even an indoor bathroom, unusual at that time in the barrio.

Mr. and Mrs. Clemente worked long and hard to give their children a good home. In his job as foreman, Mr. Clemente earned three or four dollars a week. That was not much money even then, so the Clementes did other work, too. Mr. Clemente bought an old truck and used it to carry meat and other food, which he sold door-to-door in his spare time. His truck was like a traveling grocery store. Mr. Clemente also rented the truck to local merchants and businesses.

Mrs. Clemente earned money by doing laundry at the home of the owner of the sugar-cane factory. She did not like to leave her children during the day, so she went to work in the middle of the night, when Mr. Clemente and the children were asleep.

It was the time of the Great Depression, and life was difficult in the barrio. Sugar cane was harvested from Christmastime until early summer, and most of the next year's crop was planted during the same months. During this time, the people of Carolina earned most of their small incomes, but from summer until Christmas there was no work. It was called *el tiempo muerto*—"the dead time."

During "the dead time," people in the barrio survived by growing vegetables in their gardens or keeping chickens. The chickens supplied eggs and meat, and fishing also added food to the daily diet. Mr. Clemente sold food from his truck then. Often his customers had no money to pay him, but he trusted them to pay their debts when they went back to work in the cane fields, and they always did.

The busy time began in November. That was when the harvest was ready, the planting started, and the professional baseball season opened.

For little Roberto, baseball and the sugar-cane harvest marked the beginning of each year, for they set the rhythm of life in the barrio. Clemente always remembered how the cane fields looked, smelled, and felt. As a boy, he liked to walk with his mother to the cane fields each day, when she brought her husband his lunch.

To the little boy, the fields were like a green forest. The ripe sugar cane stood about 15 feet high, and the cane-cutters moved through the fields in straight lines. "Whoosh! Whoosh!" whispered their razor-sharp machetes as they chopped down row after row of stalks.

Workdays were long and tiring during the harvest season. People in the barrio woke up early, at five or six in the morning, and by seven o'clock the laborers had finished their breakfasts of leftover rice and beans from the night before. They tied cords around the bottoms of their pants' legs, to prevent insects and snakes from biting them in the fields, then they put on broad straw hats, picked up their farm tools, and gathered along the road. Soon trucks came to take them out to the fields.

Roberto Clemente never forgot the words used by his father and the other men to describe their labors. They spoke of "doing battle" with the cane, and making a living at the work was "defending yourself." It was as if the sugar-cane fields were their enemies in a never-ending war.

At 9 o'clock in the morning the workers took a break for coffee and a piece of bread. Then the cutting continued till noon, time for lunch. This meal was very important.

While the men were in the fields, the women of Carolina spent part of the morning cooking a hot meal. At noon, each woman put the food she had cooked into three or four pots or pails. One pot held a stew made from potatoes, yams, or corn meal, with bits of chicken or fish mixed in. Another container was filled with rice, and a third one had red or white beans in a sauce. No meal was complete without rice and beans.

The workday ended by four o'clock. The men came home, where they bathed and shaved. After that it was time to relax, listen to the radio, and play baseball.

Roberto was a good child, quiet and respectful. There was only one thing that led him to be naughty or forgetful—baseball. Mrs. Clemente remembered that she had to keep him inside when the family was getting ready to go somewhere. "I would dress him up, nice and clean," she said, "and Roberto would come home full of dust and mud. I'd send him to the store on an errand, and he'd be gone for hours." Mrs. Clemente wasn't worried about Roberto, though. She knew where to find him—across the road, playing baseball.

"Roberto used to buy those rubber balls every chance he got," Mrs. Clemente said. "When he was small, he would lie in bed and bounce the ball off the walls. There were times he was so much in love with baseball that he did not want to stop playing to eat."

Roberto didn't only go to school and play ball. He helped his father on the truck and did household chores, and he was also expected to earn his own pocket money.

When he was nine years old, Roberto asked his parents for a bicycle. "You must earn the bicycle," Mr. Clemente told him, so the boy looked hard for a way to earn money. The answer came when a neighbor offered him a penny a day to work for him. Roberto's job would be to carry a milk can to the country store a half mile away, fill it, and bring it back. Roberto agreed, and did the task faithfully.

"Six o'clock every morning, I went for the milk," Clemente told a reporter years later. "I wanted to do it. I wanted to have work, to be a good man. I grew up with that on my mind." It took three years for Roberto to earn the money to pay for a used bicycle. He enjoyed riding that bicycle, because he had worked so hard for it.

The climate is warm all year in Puerto Rico, so Puerto Rican social life and games take place outdoors. People sit on their porches, playing dominoes and listening to baseball games or music, and they have cookouts and outdoor dances. The island's number-one sport is the great outdoor game, baseball.

Baseball was the best part of Roberto Clemente's childhood. "Roberto was born to be a baseball player," his mother said. Each day he ran home from the Fernandez Grammar School, drank a glass of milk and dashed outside to play. It seemed he was never without a ball in his hand. Usually, it was a rubber ball that cost only a few pennies. Whenever the ball broke or got lost, Roberto began saving his pennies for another. Meanwhile, he carried a "ball" made of crushed magazine pages wrapped in string. Night and day, he had some sort of ball in his hand. He bounced it against walls. He threw it into the air and caught it. He squeezed it, to strengthen his hands and arms. He even kept it next to him in bed at night.

Many times the boy's love of baseball got on Mrs. Clemente's nerves. One time Roberto forgot to run an important errand for his mother, and she got so annoyed that she threw his baseball bat into the wood-burning stove. Roberto cried out and snatched the bat from the flames.

When Roberto Clemente was an All-Star baseball player, he liked to tease his mother about that day, joking that she almost ruined his career. She laughed but reminded him that he had learned a lesson. "From that day on," she said, "you never failed to do your chores."

Roberto Clemente loved his parents very much. "When I was a boy," he said, "I realized what lovely people my father and mother were. I learned from them the right way to live. I never heard any hate in my house. I never heard my father or my mother raise their voices or say a bad word to each other.

"We were poor, but we never went hungry. They always found a way to feed us. My mother fed the children first, then she and my father would eat what was left," Clemente continued. "My mother had to work hard, never went to a movie, never learned to dance. But even the way we used to live, we were happy. We would sit down and make jokes and talk and eat whatever there was. That was something wonderful."

Mr. and Mrs. Clemente wanted their children to succeed in the world. They dreamed of sending them to college, but there was no money to pay for anything more than food, clothing, and shelter. Mrs. Clemente hoped Roberto would become an engineer or an architect, because he was very good in arithmetic. He also seemed to understand what made things work and was always able to fix them.

This skill stayed with Roberto Clemente all his life. Even when Clemente was a highly paid baseball player, he did all his own home repairs. "For as long as I can remember," he said, "I liked to make and fix things with my own hands."

But baseball was Roberto Clemente's greatest talent. By the time he was eight years old, he was on a real team. All the other players were two or three years older, but little Mome had no trouble making the grade. When he wasn't playing with the neighborhood team, he played baseball with his brothers. They were all talented athletes, but Roberto was the best athlete in the family.

When Roberto was a student at the Julio C. Vizarrondo High School, he was outstanding at track and field. He competed in the javelin throw, the 400-meter dash, the triple jump, and the high jump. Roberto looked like a sure bet to make the Puerto Rican Olympic team in at least one event, but he wasn't interested in the Olympics. His devotion to baseball made everything else less important.

The athletes Roberto Clemente admired were all baseball stars, and his favorite among them was Monte Irvin. Irvin, who was an outfielder for the New York Giants, played in the Puerto Rican leagues during the winter. When Roberto had 25¢ to spare and Irvin's team was playing in San Juan, the teenager took the bus to Sixto Escobar Stadium. The bus fare was five cents each way, and a seat in the bleachers cost 15¢. To sit in the sun-baked bleachers and watch his hero hit, run, and throw was Roberto's idea of a perfect day.

After the game, the boy stood outside the player's gate, waiting to see Irvin. "I never had enough nerve to look at him straight in the face," Clemente remembered. "I would wait for him to pass and then look at him. I idolized him." On August 6, 1973, Monte Irvin was inducted into baseball's Hall of Fame. On that very same day, Roberto Clemente also became a member of the Hall of Fame.

When Roberto was 14 years old, a man named Roberto Marin

spotted his outstanding ability to play baseball. Marin managed a team in the Carolina softball league. "I saw this one kid who never struck out," Marin said. "So I asked him to play for my team."

It was Roberto's first step on the road to the major leagues. He began playing for Marin's softball team, and also in the San Juan Youth Baseball League. Two years later he was starring for a San Juan team in a league that was at the level of Class A professional baseball in the United States.

By the time he was 17, Clemente's play caught the attention of Alex Campanis, a scout for the Brooklyn Dodgers. Roberto was one of 72 young hopefuls at a major-league tryout at Escobar Stadium. Campanis had all of them catch and throw from the outfield, then he had them sprint 60 yards. After the last dash, Campanis said, "Thank you, and good-bye" to 71 of them.

The only one left was Roberto Clemente. Campanis sent a minor-league pitcher to the mound and asked Clemente to bat against him. "The kid hit line drives all over the place," Campanis said, "while I'm behind the batting cage telling myself, we've got to sign him. The kid swings with both feet off the ground and hits drives to right and sharp ground balls up the middle. How could I miss him? He was the greatest natural athlete I ever saw as a free agent!"

Roberto Clemente had everything a major-league team looks for. He had a strong arm, he ran fast, and he was a solid hitter. Equally important, he was a serious young man who was eager to learn and improve. Clemente lacked just one thing: professional experience.

On the advice of Roberto Marin, the teenager signed a contract to play winter baseball with a team called the Santurce Crabbers. They played in the Double-A Puerto Rican league. The Crabbers were stocked with seasoned pros from the U.S. major leagues and other promising rookies like Clemente. It was exactly the experience Roberto needed.

Baseball Greats

In the spring of 1954, after two fine seasons with Santurce, 19-year-old Roberto Clemente's career took a leap upward. He was signed by the Montreal Royals of the International League, only one step below the major leagues. The next year, Clemente took the biggest step of all when he joined the Pittsburgh Pirates of the National League.

For the next 18 years, Clemente made his mark in the record books. He won the National League batting title four times. He won 12 Gold Glove awards for fielding excellence. He was voted the National League's Most Valuable Player and the World Series MVP in 1971. He also played in 12 All-Star games. Clemente's list of baseball records goes on and on, capped by his joining a select group of players with 3,000 or more hits in their major-league careers.

If his achievements as a player were Roberto Clemente's only claim to fame, they would be enough, but there is much more to this man's story. Clemente was not only a notable baseball player; he was also a great human being.

No matter how successful he became or how much money he made, Clemente remained the same down-to-earth person. He worked hard at his sport, didn't drink liquor or smoke, and stayed up late only when Pittsburgh played a night game. Otherwise, like the sugar-cane workers of Carolina, he was in bed by 10 p.m.

Roberto Clemente's whole life was baseball, his wife and children, and giving to others. Friends in Puerto Rico always turned to him when they needed help, and he came through for them. Every winter, he conducted youth baseball clinics all over Puerto Rico, and he regularly visited sick children in hospitals. He took part in anti-drug campaigns and led an effort to build a large sports complex for Puerto Rican boys and girls.

On December 23, 1972, a terrible earthquake rocked the country of Nicaragua. Clemente immediately rushed to help, and he went on Puerto Rican radio and television, asking for medicine, food, and clothing for the earthquake survivors. Then he chartered several planes to carry these supplies to Nicaragua. Wanting to make sure that the supplies reached the neediest people, he decided to go along with the crew aboard the last plane. He left San Juan on New Year's Eve and never returned. Clemente's plane fell into the sea, killing everyone aboard.

The shock of Clemente's sudden, tragic death was felt by people everywhere. To Puerto Ricans, it was the loss of a national hero. To his family it was the loss of a husband, a father, a son, a brother. To baseball fans, it was the loss of a superstar. To everyone who learned of his acts of kindness, it was the loss of a fine human being.

The summer after his death, Roberto Clemente was inducted into the Baseball Hall of Fame. On this occasion, friends remembered something he had once said: "I want to be remembered as a ballplayer who gave all he had to give." Roberto Clemente got his wish, for that is exactly how he is remembered.

INDEX

American League, 25
Athletics, Philadelphia, 17

Baseball Hall of Fame, 16, 25, 36, 50, 58, 61
Black Barons, 47, 48
Braves, Boston, 15
Bush, Guy, 15, 16

Clemente, Roberto, 51–61
   childhood, 52–58
   high school, 58
   major-league career, 51, 59–61
   minor league, 59
   MVP, 60
   parents, 52–57
   siblings, 53
Cleveland, Grover, School, 32–34
Columbia University, 22–24
Commerce, High School of, 23, 24
Cubs, Chicago, 7

Davis, Piper, 47, 48
Dodgers, Brooklyn, 27, 34, 35, 36, 47, 49, 59
Dunn, Jack, 14, 15
Durocher, Leo, 49

Earnshaw, George, 17, 18
Escobar Stadium, 58, 59

Forbes Field, 15

Gehrig, Lou, 17–26
   Appreciation Day, 25, 26
   at Columbia University, 23, 24
   childhood, 18–21
   chores, 21
   dependability, 22
   disease, 25
   high school, 23
   home runs, 17, 18, 24, 25
   "Iron Horse," 22, 25, 26
   major-league career, 17, 18, 24–26

   MVP, 25
   parents, 18–23, 24, 25
   "Pride of the Yankees," 26
   retirement, 25
   school, 19, 21, 22, 23
   sports, 19–21, 23, 24
   standards, 22
Giants, New York, 48, 49
Giants, San Francisco, 51
Great Depression, 42, 54

Hall of Fame, Baseball, 16, 25, 36, 50, 58, 61

Industrial League, 43, 44, 47

Kane, Harry, 23, 24

Lucas, Red, 15

Mack, Connie, 17, 18
Mahaffey, Roy, 17, 18
Marin, Roberto, 58, 59
Maris, Roger, 14
Matthias, Brother, 12–14
Mays, Willie, 39–50
   childhood, 40–46
   high school, 48
   home runs, 49
   major-league career, 47, 49, 50
   minor-league career, 46–49
   natural ability, 39, 43
   parents, 39–48
   semi-professional, 46
Mets, New York, 49
Monarchs, Kansas City, 35
Most Valuable Player, 25, 36, 60

National League, 36, 48, 49, 60
Negro Leagues, 35, 47, 48
New York City, 18, 23

Orioles, Baltimore, 14

Pirates, Pittsburgh, 15, 16, 51, 60
pokenins, 12
Puerto Rican League, 58, 59

Red Sox, 14
Red Sox, Boston, 15
Racism, 27, 28, 29, 31, 36, 37
Rickey, Branch, 35, 36
Robinson, Jackie, 27–37, 47
   army, 35
   childhood, 28–34
   college, 35
   education, 33–35
   major-league career, 27, 28, 34–36
   move to California, 29, 30
   MVP, 36
   Negro Leagues, 35, 47
   parents, 28–30, 31, 32
   siblings, 28, 30, 32, 34, 35
Robinson, Mack, 28, 34, 35
Royals, Montreal, 36
Ruth, George (Babe) Herman, 7–16, 17, 25, 26, 49
   and Brother Matthias, 12–14
   appetite, 12
   childhood, 8, 9
   generosity, 12
   Hall of Fame, 16
   home runs, 8, 14, 16
   learns baseball, 12
   learns shirtmaking, 13
   major-league career, 7, 8, 14–16
   nicknamed "Babe," 15
   parents, 8, 9
   sibling, 8
   St. Mary's education, 10–14
   schoolwork, 11–13

St. Mary's Industrial School, 9–15
   baseball, 11–14
   Catholic brothers, 10–14
   routine, 10, 11
   sports, 11–14

Yankees, New York, 7, 8, 14, 15, 17, 24, 25
Yankee Stadium, 25

World Olympics, 34
World Series, 7, 8, 60
Wrigley Field, 8, 23